Hot Air Balloons

Written by Anne Myers

STECK-VAUGHN
COMPANY
ELEMENTARY · SECONDARY · ADULT · LIBRARY

Birds can fly high in the sky.
People have always wanted to fly, too.
The first time that anyone flew was in
a hot air balloon.
Do you know how the balloon flew?

2

Two French brothers made the first balloon.
Their balloon was made of cloth and paper.
They tied a basket below to hold passengers.
A sheep, a duck, and a rooster were the first
to fly in the balloon.

3

People were amazed to see the balloon fly.
It landed with the animals safe inside.
Then people wanted to fly in balloons.
The first balloon to carry people flew
over Paris, France.

The first balloons were filled with hot smoke.
Large fires were built on the ground.
The hot air made the balloons rise.
Then they floated in the air for about
thirty minutes.

More people began to fly in hot air balloons.
People who flew them were called pilots.
Other people just wanted to take rides.
These passengers rode in the basket along
with the pilot.

Hot air balloons had one big problem.
The hot air inside them cooled off.
This made the balloons come down.
Then burners were put under the balloons.
They kept the air hot, so balloons flew longer.

Flying hot air balloons became very popular.
People gathered to watch the balloons fly.
Some fairs started to have balloon rides.
Children even played with toy balloons.

8

Today hot air balloons are still popular.
They are very bright and colorful.
They come in many shapes and sizes.
Some are even taller than a seven-story building.

Balloons today are made of nylon cloth.
Their ropes are made of steel.
They all have a burner under them.
They usually have a basket underneath
to carry passengers.

Here's how a balloon begins its flight.
First, it is spread out on the ground.
A fan fills the balloon with air.
Then the burner warms the air
inside the balloon.

The warm air makes the balloon rise.
Then everyone gets in the basket.
A blast of hot air lifts the balloon.
Slowly, it rises up into the sky.

12

Once in the sky, balloons can move fast.
But most flights are usually quiet and slow.
They last for about one or two hours.
Hot air balloons float high above the ground.

To land, the pilot looks for a large, open area.
The pilot pulls a line tied to the balloon.
This line lets the hot air out the top.
Then the balloon floats down.

14

Down, down the balloon floats.
A balloon landing can be very rough.
The basket may bump along the ground.
Or it may tip over onto its side.

 15

The view from a hot air balloon is amazing.
And a ride in a hot air balloon is exciting.
Balloons fly with the wind and float in the clouds.
Would you like to take a hot air balloon ride?